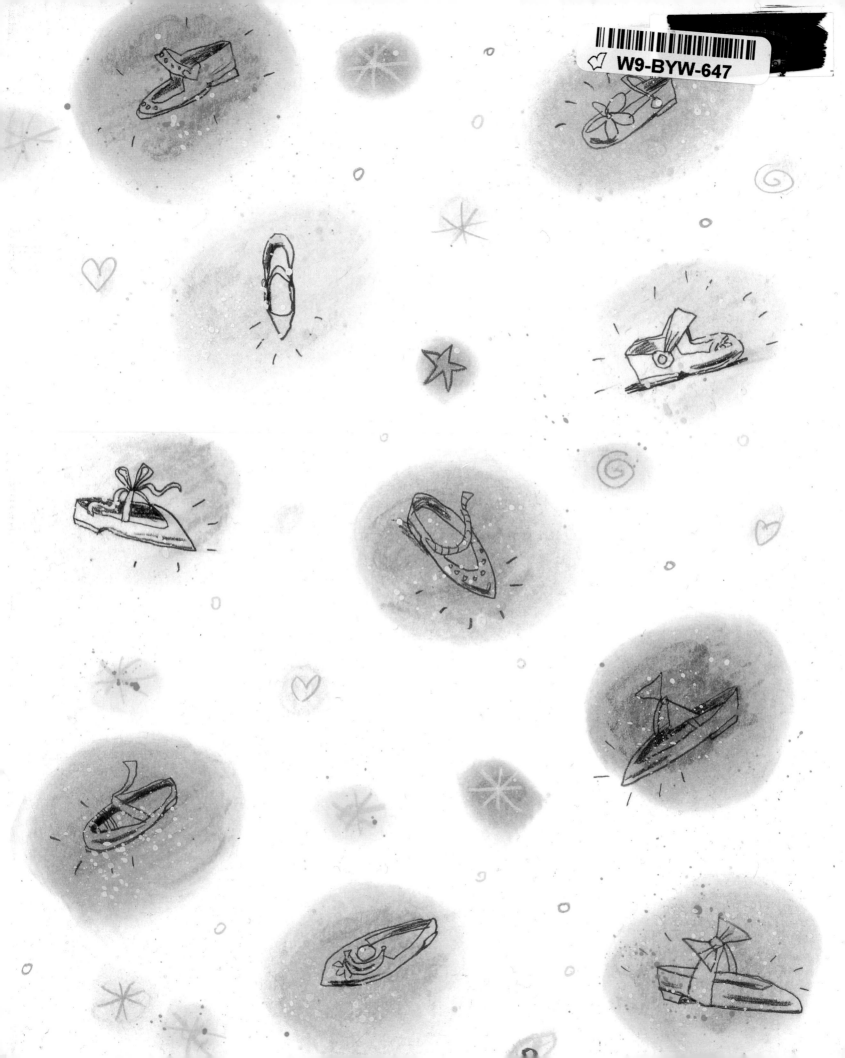

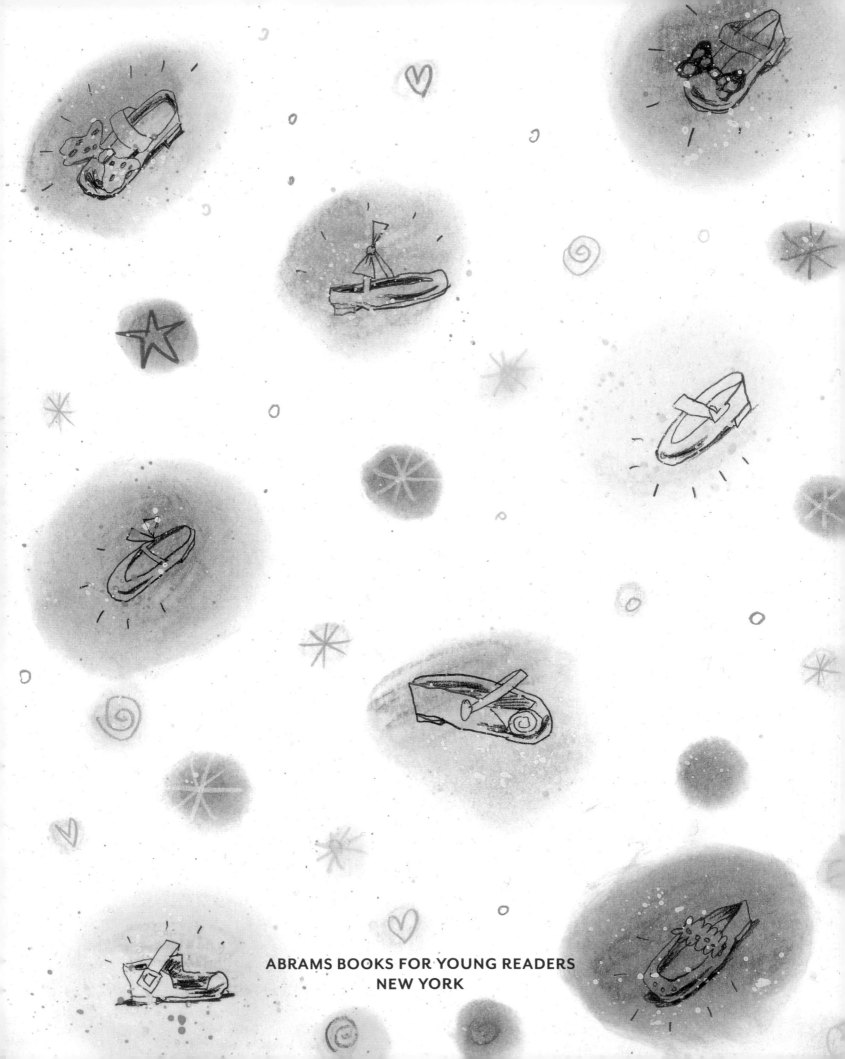

ABRAMS BOOKS FOR YOUNG READERS
NEW YORK

I'm Gonna Climb a Mountain in My Patent Leather Shoes

by Marilyn Singer   Illustrated by Lynne Avril

For that patent-leather-shoe
mountain climber Amy Livingston
—M. S.

The art for this book was created with pastel chalk and matte medium with pencil outline.

For Olivia
—L. A.

*Many thanks to Steve Aronson, Donn Livingston, my wonderful agent Brenda Bowen,
my fabulous editor Tamar Brazis, and the good folks at Abrams. —M. S.*

Library of Congress Cataloging-in-Publication Data

Singer, Marilyn.
I'm gonna climb a mountain in my patent leather shoes / by Marilyn Singer ; illustrated by Lynne Avril.
pages cm
Summary: Sadie is all girl, but she does not let that—or her wardrobe—stop her from enjoying a family camping
trip as she helps pitch the tent in "fancy ruffled pants" and looks for Bigfoot while wearing a tutu.
ISBN 978-1-4197-0336-2
[1. Stories in rhyme. 2. Camping—Fiction. 3. Sex role—Fiction. 4. Brothers and sisters—Fiction.] I. Avril, Lynne,
1961—illustrator. II. Title.
PZ8.3.S6154Ik 2014
2013042474

Printed and bound in China
10 9 8 7 6 5 4 3 2 1

Abrams Books for Young Readers are available at special discounts when purchased in quantity for premiums
and promotions as well as fundraising or educational use. Special editions can also be created to specification.
For details, contact specialsales@abramsbooks.com or the address below.

ABRAMS
THE ART OF BOOKS SINCE 1949
115 West 18th Street
New York, NY 10011
www.abramsbooks.com

Today we're going camping.

Can't wait till we get there!

I'm thrilled about the things we'll do . . .

...and what I'm gonna wear!

I'm gonna climb a mountain in my patent leather shoes.

I'm looking in my closet—so many things to choose.

"Please hurry, Sadie," says my mom. "We've got no time to lose."

I'm gonna climb a mountain

'in my patent leather shoes.

with my sparkly new suitcase.

I've got my lacy socks on and a big smile on my face.

My brother tells me, "Sadie! You take up too much space!"

I'm riding in the car now with my sparkly new suitcase.

I'm helping pitch our pup tent in my fancy ruffled pants.

My brother yells, "Hey, Sadie, be careful of those ants!"

I holler back, "And you watch out for poison ivy plants!"

I'm helping pitch our pup tent

in my fancy ruffled pants.

I'm looking out for Bigfoot

I'm looking out for Bigfoot in my ballerina skirt.

He can call me pesky; he can call me Squirt.

Sticks and stones may break my bones, but names will never hurt.

in my ballerina skirt.

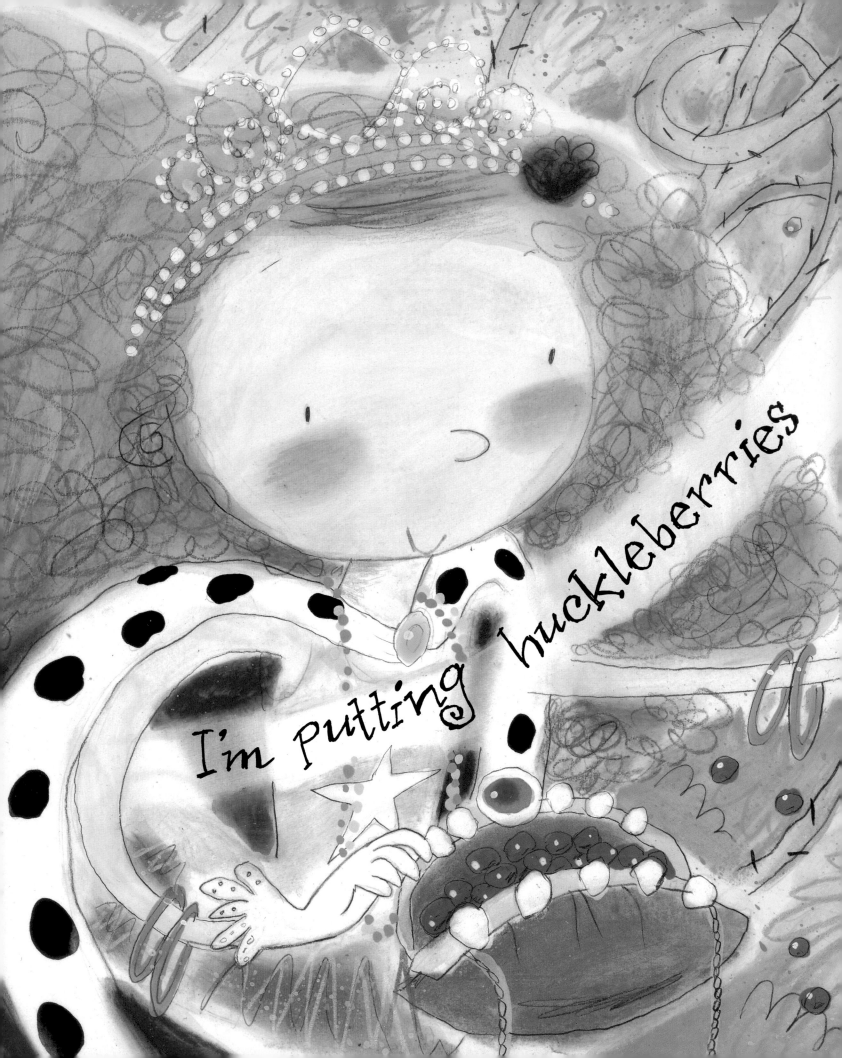

in my purple party bag.

Even with the prickles and other things that snag,

I'm faster than my brother—I've got a right to brag!

I'm putting huckleberries in my purple party bag.

I'm hunting down a chipmunk

in my royal satin cape.

He ran off with my berries. I can't let him escape!

My brother hoots and bounds around—he's acting like an ape!

I'm hunting down a chipmunk in my royal satin cape.

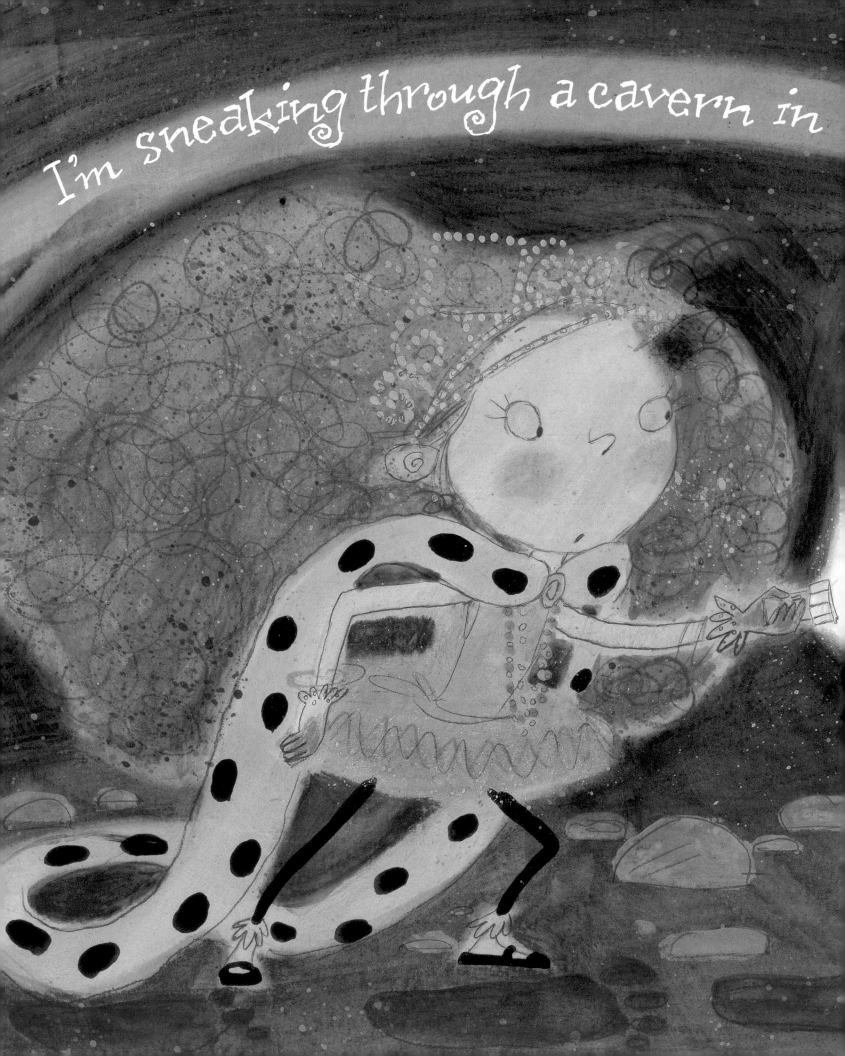

my gloves that once were white.

The chipmunk's gone. I'm dirty. I just turned on a light.

I see a spider on my left. Is Bigfoot on my right?

I'm sneaking through a cavern in my gloves that once were white.

I'm climbing up a mountain in my patent leather shoes.

My brother's just ahead of me. He's looking out for clues.

I think someone's behind us. I hear a voice, but whose?

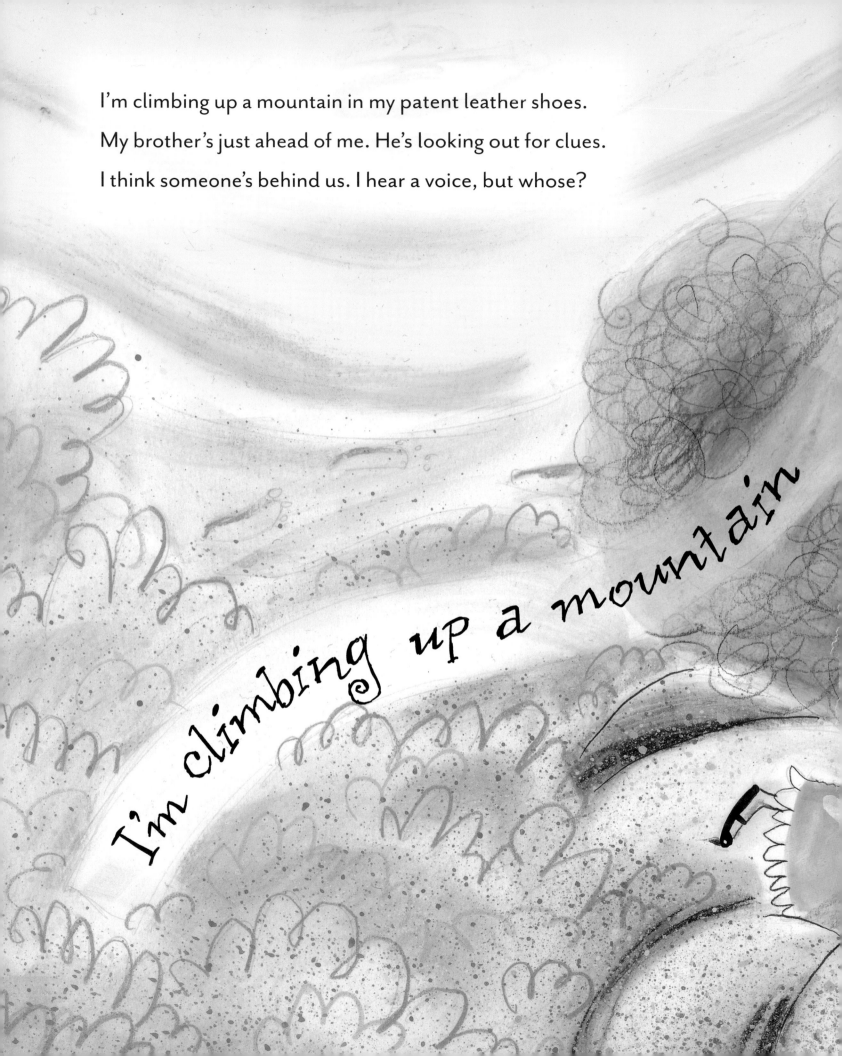

I'm climbing up a mountain

in my patent leather shoes.

I'm swimming in the river

in my flowered underwear.

Bigfoot might be after me, but right now I don't care.

If he forgot his bathing suit, I'll offer him a pair.

I'm swimming in the river in my flowered underwear.

Could I capture Bigfoot with my seven strings of pearls?

Lasso him and tie him up with just a few quick twirls?

My brother thinks that boys are brave. I've told him, "So are girls!"

Could I capture Bigfoot with

my seven strings of pearls?

I'm ruling by the fire

...in my shiny silver crown.

My brother's playing Bigfoot with a growl and a frown.

I pretend to drive him off. We both jump up and down!

I'm ruling by the fire in my shiny silver crown.

I'm saving us from Bigfoot

"Begone!" I tell his shadow. "Get lost!" I boldly scold.

My brother's got the shivers. He says that's 'cause he's cold.

I'm saving us from Bigfoot with my magic wand of gold!

with my magic wand of gold!

I'm watching all the stars shine

I'm watching all the stars shine in my pink pj's with feet.

"Let's watch all night," my brother says. "All night!" I repeat.

We'll wake up in the morning when birds begin to tweet.

in my pink pj's with feet.

I went and climbed a mountain in my patent leather shoes.

I swam a river, chased a monster—have you heard the news?

If I had to do it over, you know what I would choose?

I'd climb ANOTHER mountain

in my patent leather shoes!

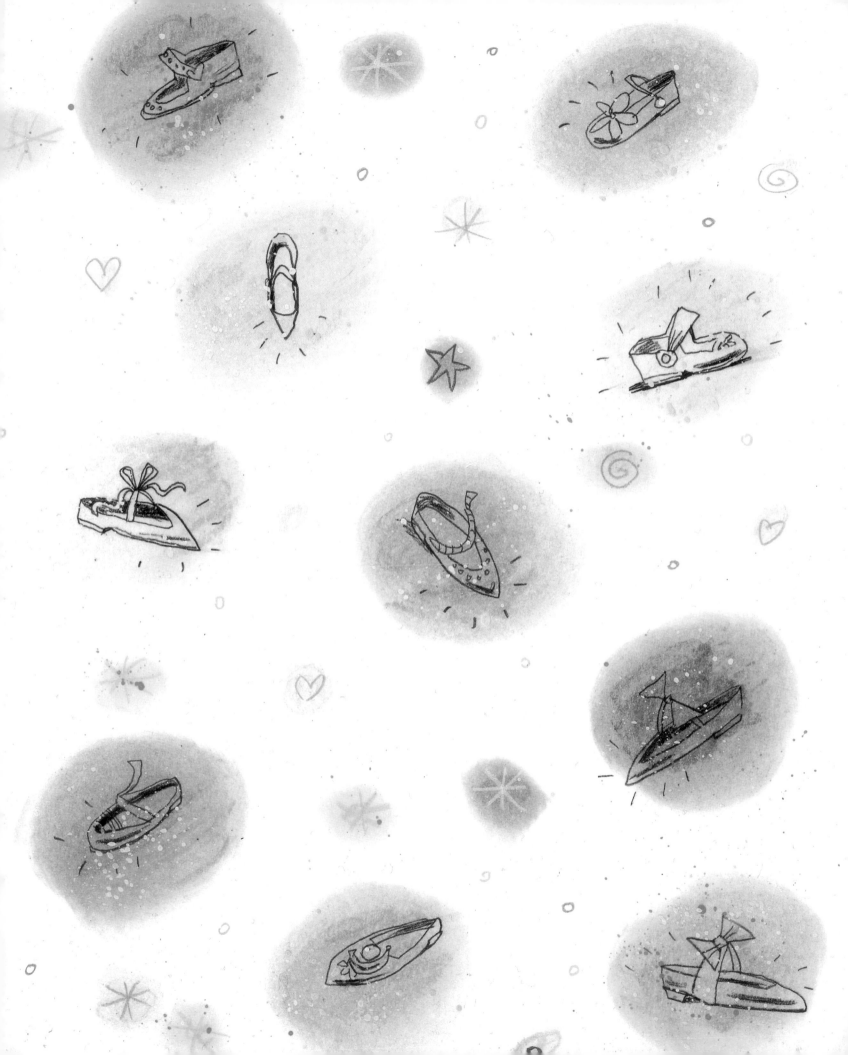

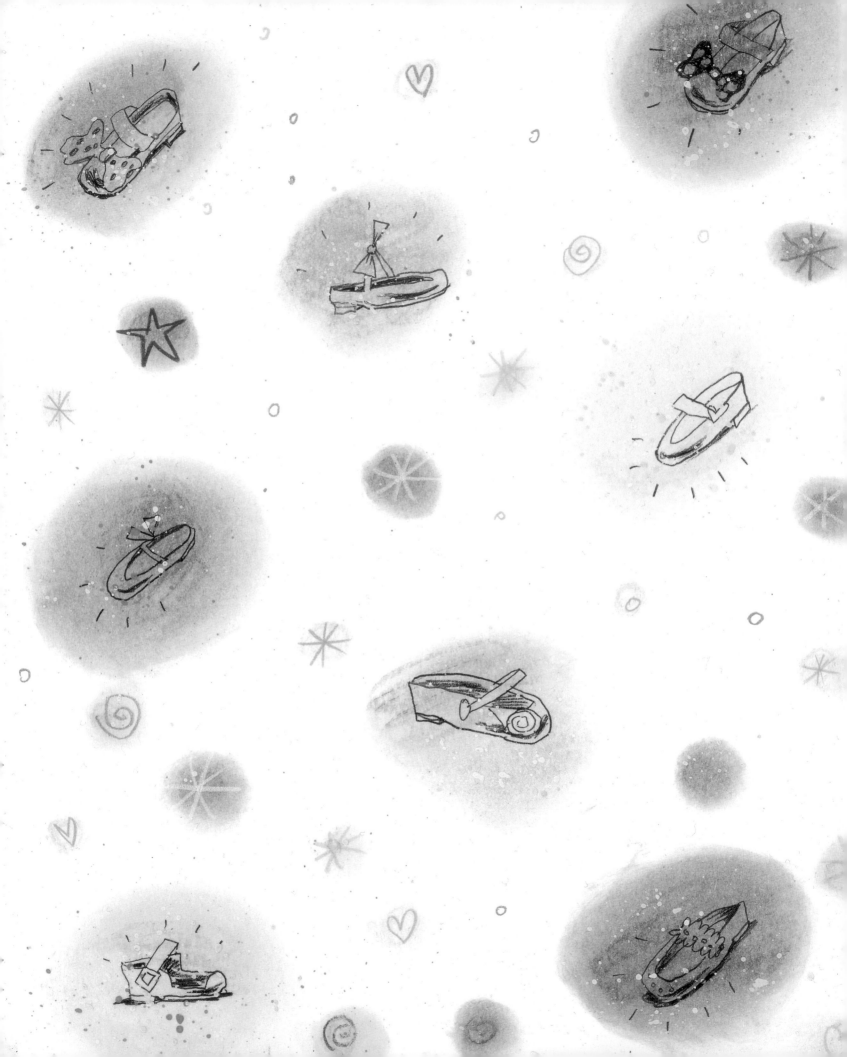